BEANIE
AND HIS PONY

by Ruth and Latrobe Carroll

Cover illustration by Nada Serafimovic and Ruth Carroll

Cover design by Elle Staples

First published in 1957

Originally titled *Tough Enough's Pony*

This unabridged version has updated grammar and spelling.

© 2019 Jenny Phillips

www.thegoodandthebeautiful.com

To
Patricia Cummings, for all the
help she has given us.

And we want to thank Tom Alexander
of the Cataloochee Ranch, and
Captain Dan Yeomans and Marguerite
and Floyd Yeomans, of Harkers
Island, for invaluable assistance.

Table of Contents

Chapter One 1

Chapter Two 19

Chapter Three 34

Chapter Four 48

Chapter Five 66

Chapter One

All of a sudden, Beanie Tatum stood still. He had heard a distant barking. "Something's happened!" he called out to his brothers and sisters. "That's Tough Enough barking and barking back over yonder. He's barking his *something's-happened* way."

Beanie began to run toward the sounds his dog was making. They were coming from behind a sand dune some distance away, a dune shaped like an enormous wave.

His brothers and sisters were running, too. But the five young Tatums had never run so slowly. Their feet kept sinking into dry sand. It wasn't the kind of running they had ever done before. They were used to hard-dirt trails near the Tatum farm in the Great Smoky Mountains, hundreds and hundreds of miles away in the West. Now they were visiting their great-grandparents on Shackleford Banks, a long, skinny, lonesome island off the coast of North Carolina.

All of Beanie's brothers and sisters were older than he was, so they were running faster. Irby was in the lead because he had been nearest to the dune when the barking began. Buck, the oldest, was far behind Irby. But he was gradually catching up because his legs were the longest. Behind him came Serena. And behind Serena, and only a step or two in front of Beanie, was Annie Mae.

Tough Enough's barking was going on and on. What was he barking at? Every second, in Beanie's ears, that yiping sounded just a little louder because Beanie was just a little nearer.

Now Beanie had reached the base of the dune. The four others were already climbing it. "Wish I could run faster," he told himself. "It's sure hard going. Land's alive! I feel just like an old fly stuck in a puddle of molasses."

He had to keep turning from side to side as the branches of dead trees kept barring his way. The great dune looked motionless, but it really was a moving thing. Under the sweep of strong winds from the sea, it had been creeping slowly inland, day after day, year after year—pushing into a forest of cedars and water oaks and myrtles. Gray, naked trunks and limbs stuck out of the smothering sand. The dune was a graveyard of trees.

Irby was the first to reach the top. Beanie saw him standing rigid, staring down at something on the other side.

For a few seconds Irby didn't say a word. Then he shouted, "Looky! *Looky*!"

Beanie finally scrambled to the top. He stared hard.

He was looking down at a young pony. It was a Banker pony, one of the hundreds that ran wild on the Outer Banks of North Carolina. The colt was lying motionless, stretched out in a hollow in the shade of a gnarled cedar tree. Close beside him, Tough Enough was still yiping away.

"Is he—is he—dead?" said Beanie.

Tough Enough ran up to Beanie. He gave a small asking whimper and halted with one foot raised. He started off again, ran all around the pony, then crept close to him. He put his nose down and sniffed at the pony's left hind leg. Pretty soon he touched the leg with an investigative paw.

The colt kicked out at Tough Enough. It was a feeble kick, but Beanie's voice went up in a shout, "He's alive!"

All the young Tatums went close to the pony. He was very thin. His hip bone stuck up out of his hollow flank. His brown coat was ragged and dull-looking; it was dark with sweat. His sunken eyes looked sad. They looked as if nothing mattered to him, nothing in the world.

"Poor pony," Beanie said. He felt as if he *were* the pony, lying helpless on the sand.

Serena said, "Looky! His left hind leg is swollen."

"I reckon he hurt it," said Annie Mae.

Buck said, "He must be one of Great Grandpa's ponies. He's got Great Grandpa's brand on him."

Buck pointed to the mark a branding iron had left on the pony's flank, a mark shaped like the letter *P*. That was the first letter of Great Grandpa's last name—*P* for Piggott, Captain John Piggott.

Serena said, "Great Grandpa's the one who'd know how to make him well again. Let's fetch Great Grandpa."

"But I'm wondering," said Buck, "wondering if Great Grandpa's stout enough to come all the way here. It's a far piece from his fishing camp—far for him."

Serena said, "Our great grandpa's mighty old, but he's mighty pert." She smiled and looked proud.

"Well, anyhow," Buck said, "I'll run and ask him if he can come."

Beanie told Buck, "Better bring back a pail of water. The pony's mighty thirsty, that's for certain."

Buck nodded. He started to run toward the Piggott fishing camp. The camp was an old cottage, about three miles away, on the Sound side of Shackleford Banks. The Piggotts had taken the Tatums there because the swimming and fishing were better than on Harkers Island, across the Sound, where the Piggotts' home was.

Beanie looked at some grass growing nearby. "I'll pull some of that grass for the pony," he said. "Looks like he needs some bad; he's so thin and starving-like."

"Maybe he'll eat some of the sea oats yonder," said Serena. She was looking at a cluster of graceful stems topped by pale green seed pods.

The four young Tatums scattered to get sea oats and grass.

For once, Tough Enough didn't follow Beanie. He sat close to the colt's head, licking the colt's muzzle. The pony didn't try to move his head away. His eyes had changed. Their glazed, half-dead look was partly gone. Now they seemed deeper. Warmer.

The boys and girls brought sea oats and grass. One by one, hopefully, they offered them to the pony.

His nostrils twitched, his eyes brightened still more. Once his parched lips opened slightly. He was trying to eat. But in a moment they closed.

Beanie and His Pony

The young Tatums looked sad.

"Let's pile it all close to his nose," said Serena, "so he'll smell it every time he breathes in."

"Let's!" Beanie said eagerly. "Later on, maybe he'll perk up a bit and eat some."

So they heaped the grass and sea oats just in front of the pony's muzzle.

Pretty soon they heard a shout. It came from Buck. He was walking beside Great Grandpa, carrying a pail of water. Captain Piggott was trudging slowly, helping himself along with a stout stick. A corncob pipe stuck out of one side of his mouth.

"I'm slower than a beat-up old barge getting pushed upstream," the Captain called out. "But I'll make yonder port with you all directly."

Tough Enough left the pony. He went racing to meet Buck and the Captain. He ran around and around them, looking up. Now and then he would give a short bark, as if telling them to hurry. Then he ran back to the pony. He sat down close to his head.

Pretty soon the Captain was looking at the colt. He took his pipe from his mouth, knocked out hot ashes, and put it in his pocket. "Well-l-l," he said, drawing the word out long and thin, "what's this?" His voice was calm and kind. "Mighty puny-looking pony. He's bad off—nothing but bones and hide."

He put his hand on the colt's back, on his forehead, on his flank. With gentle fingertips, he touched the swollen leg. The pony lay still except when he twitched his skin to shake off a pestering fly.

"Looky!" Beanie said in a quick, happy voice. "He feels pert enough to jerk his hide."

The Captain had seen the brand on the pony's flank. "Well-l-l, now!" he said. "It's Sassy Boy! Sure enough. Little old Sassy."

He looked at the young Tatums. "That's the name your great grandma and I gave this little fellow when he was just a foal. He was mighty sassy. Mighty pesky, when a bunch of boys rounded up the herd and drove the little horses into a corral when we had a pony penning. We had a time with him. The shines he cut, kicking and using his teeth! He pulled a button off my pants pocket behind. He pulled buttons off the pants of some of the boys, and once the seat of the pants went with the button. We tied him to a post, but he nibbled and pulled at the rope till it broke; then off he ran to his ma. Other foals were plumb tuckered out after the penning. But not Sassy, not him."

Great Grandpa stopped speaking. He peered at the five young listening faces. He nodded. "Sassy must be about a year old now—a yearling. Yes, sir. That's Sassy, sure as I got shoes on."

"Sassy," Beanie repeated. His voice was warm. It lingered on the name.

"Well," said the Captain, "he isn't Sassy now." He looked at the pony. "Let's see if he'll drink."

Great Grandpa lifted the pony's head and held it up. Buck tilted the bucket so the water touched Sassy's nose.

The pony drank a little and coughed weakly, then drank a few sips more.

Great Grandpa said, "Reckon that's all the water we can stow away in him now. Matter-of-fact, it would be mighty bad for him to guzzle down a sudden slew of water. And now let's see if he'll eat any of that grass and sea oats you young-uns piled up."

Beanie offered the pony some sea grass and then some sea oats. But still the pony wouldn't eat.

"Well," said Great Grandpa, "maybe it's milk he's hankering for. Now I'll see if I can find out what's mommucking the little fellow."

He took hold of the colt's left leg and bent it up so he could see the bottom of the hoof. He held the hoof a while, studying and studying it. The pony didn't move.

"Sassy's got a real bad foot," the Captain said at last. "There's infection in there, right considerable. It's given him a fever."

"Fever," said Beanie. The word hurt.

"What happened to his foot, Great Grandpa?" Irby asked.

The Captain said, "I reckon he stepped down hard on something small and sharp. Most likely a piece of broken shell. Anyways, the sharp thing went up into his hoof. I can see a little slit there. He got graveled—that's what we call it. And then some dirt must have worked its way up, and that finished the business—the bad business."

The Captain took out his long-bladed pocket knife. He sterilized the blade by holding it to the flame of a match. Beanie looked at it, and then he looked at Sassy. A small shiver ran through him.

The Captain gave him a steady look. "Beanie, don't you go getting down in the mouth. The thing I'm going to do won't hurt Sassy much. He isn't the first graveled pony I've fixed up, not by a long sight, he isn't. And remember, it's *got* to be done."

Great Grandfather told the boys to hold the pony in case he struggled. He began to cut into Sassy's left hind hoof, starting at the small slit he had found. The pony seemed to know that Captain Piggott was helping him. He kept very still.

Great Grandfather scraped out a little sand and mud. "Can't get *at* the pesky thing, whatever it is," he

Beanie and His Pony

said. "It's worked itself so far up that it must have been in there a long time."

He washed out the wound with turpentine. He said, "When Buck told me about the little horse, I figured I'd better bring this bottle of germ-killer, just in case."

He waited a little while. Then he pulled a piece of raveled rope from one of his pockets. He stuffed the hemp up into the cut, packing it firmly.

He said, "That'll keep the infected place clean and keep dirt from getting in. Reckon we've done all we can for now. After quite a while, the sharp shell, or whatever it is, will work its way up close to the top of his hoof, and we'll see a kind of raw place there. When that happens, I'll cut down into the hoof and pull the thing plumb out."

Beanie kept looking at the pony. He couldn't look enough. "If he'll just only get well and strong," he said to himself. "And then, if Great Grandpa would just give him to us, and we could take him back…back home to our farm."

It was a dazzling thought. Beanie could see the Tatum farm again. He could see it in his mind. The old log cabin, a soft weathered gray. Green fields sloping steeply around it. Mountains rising tall and proud behind.

The Tatums had gone away from there. Away in their old truck, rattling and wheezing and chugging. Through Beanie's mind, like a motion picture run off at a fast speed, went their trip: the journey from the mountains, down, down, down toward the sea—down to stay with the young Tatums' great-grandparents, Captain John Piggott and Lizzie Lou Piggott.

A faint, scratchy sound pulled Beanie back to the here and now. Great Grandfather was rubbing his chin, stroking it thoughtfully. "We'd best be getting back on home to the camp," he said. "It'll be a snail-worrying trip for me. Got to navigate there in time for supper."

"Supper!" said Buck.

"Supper!" said Irby.

And Tough Enough knew what that word meant. He wagged his tail and barked. He ran his tongue over his damp nose and made it damper.

"Aye, aye," said the Captain with a slow smile. "Supper. There's no word quite as good, excepting 'breakfast' and 'dinner.' Well, let's go see what my Lizzie Lou and your ma are cooking up. Something mighty fine, most likely."

Beanie and Buck and Irby and Serena and Annie Mae started off with the Captain. But Tough Enough didn't follow them. He trotted to the top of the small hillock a few yards away from Sassy. He sat there on his haunches. His large ears were up; his nostrils quivered as he sniffed the air. Quite plainly, he was sure he had a job, the watchdog job of guarding the sick pony.

Beanie turned around. He called out, "Here Tough Enough—here Tough—come on, Tough."

Tough Enough sprang to his feet, but he went hurrying to Sassy. He snapped at a fly that was buzzing round the pony's neck and caught it in his mouth. His jaw moved up and down, his throat twitched in a swallowing way. Only then did he get up and follow, slow and sidling, as if part of him wanted to come but most of him wanted to stay there with Sassy.

Chapter Two

When Pa Tatum heard that Tough Enough had found a pony, he slapped his leg and laughed his biggest laugh. "That little old flea-bit, into-everything hound!" he shouted.

Ma Tatum pursed her lips. "Well, now, I *never*!"

She looked hard at Beanie. "Young man, don't you go getting any notions about adding a pony to your zoo. You already have a dog, a kitty, a talking crow, a raccoon, and a fixed skunk. And what about all the hermit crabs you're keeping? Law me! It gives a body a turn to see those shells a-walking round like they were bewitched. Last night, before I got to sleep, I could

hear them a-scraping and a-scratching over the floor. After supper you take those poor critters back to the beach where you found them. And then you feed that zoo of yours."

Beanie hung his head. The hermit crabs had such pretty shells. They poked out such funny red legs. He wanted to study them a while, but he knew his mother was right. "It is kind of mean to keep them in the house," he admitted.

He had let his raccoon and his skunk and his talking crow go free soon after he and his family had come to the island. Wild creatures ought to run loose, he felt. It was cruel to cage them or tether them up indoors.

Beanie swallowed down his chowder, his fried mullet and beans and biscuits and apple pie, without really tasting them. His mind wasn't on his supper; it was on his pets. It was on the crabs. It was on the sick pony.

After supper he put the crabs back near the water's edge.

Then he put a pan of table scraps and a pan of water out near the back door. Tough Enough was there, waiting with a fast-moving tail. He gobbled up his supper in a hurry, with small smacking noises. And the kitten, Bobcat Bob, was waiting, too. His fuzzy button of a tail was up and as straight as he could hold it. He said, "Prrrr." He rubbed and rubbed his side against Beanie's leg. Quietly and daintily he began to eat.

Beanie heard a whirr of wings. Something heavy landed WUP on his shoulder. It was the talking crow.

"Lands!" he gasped. "Midnight, you plumb scared me!"

He lifted his hand and stroked the glossy feathers on the bird's back. "Hey, hey, hey!" the crow said loudly, right in Beanie's ear. Then he made some noises like hoarse squawky words, "Hurry back real soon!" He gave a scratchy chuckle. Beanie picked up a scrap of apple and gave it to him. The big bird went flapping off with it.

Not far away, a small, striped face was poking out between tall blades of grass. It was Beanie's skunk, Sweetie Pie. She trotted toward Beanie with delicate steps. He reached down and smoothed her lustrous fur and her soft fur tail. She arched herself and made pleased sounds in her throat. Side by side with the kitten, she nosed into the food pan.

Down from a stunted yaupon tree dropped a raccoon. Fat Stuff was his name. He waddled toward his supper in greedy haste.

"Sakes alive!" Beanie said. "It's like each critter's got a watch. Reckon there's nothing like a stomach to tell the time of day."

Supper time was the only time Beanie ever saw the skunk and the raccoon, because they slept during the daylight hours.

Beanie laughed out loud. He was looking at the raccoon. Fat Stuff was washing his food in the pan of water, just as he usually did. He was busy with a biscuit. It dripped soggily, oozing out between his small dark fingers. He stared at his empty paws.

Great Grandma opened the back door. She handed Beanie a long-necked bottle. It had a white mixture in it: half water, half canned milk, and a teaspoonful of molasses.

"Here's Sassy's supper," she said. "Just take hold of his lower lip at a corner of his mouth and pull it out till it makes a funnel. Lift his head up. Then hold the neck of the bottle between his front and back teeth, and let the milk run down into his mouth. Better take Irby along to help."

Beanie and Irby started off, with Tough Enough running on ahead.

The brothers made their way along the beach. The waters of the Sound rippled against the shore. The sea wind was singing a little lonesome song. Beanie could hear faintly the thunder of the surf on the other side of the island, the Atlantic Ocean side. He liked its strange soft booming.

He and Irby followed a dry white trail, a path of dimples in the sand that many feet had made. On one side, cedars and wax myrtles and water oaks were crouching strangely, as if they knew their lives depended on keeping down out of the strong salt winds from the sea. The great dune towered above them, threatening every green thing.

"Yonder's the pony tree," said Beanie.

The colt was lying just as they had left him, under the twisted cedar. Tough Enough was with him. When a breeze brought Beanie's scent, the dog's ears went up. He licked his nose, and he wiggled it. He barked.

Beanie and Irby began to give the pony his supper.

"Drink it all up, now," Beanie said to him gently. "It's real tasty. It'll start you getting well."

Fast and eager, with greedy little noises, Sassy swallowed the mixture.

Pretty soon Beanie was smiling his biggest smile. The bottle was empty. The milk and water and molasses were inside Sassy.

Beanie stroked and stroked the pony. "Just wait," he said. "You'll be frisking around just as good as new, stomping and kicking up your heels. Just wait. You just wait."

He put his hand flat against the pony's neck. He held it there. Sassy's coat still felt too hot. Fever-hot.

He gave the colt three goodbye pats. He said, "You won't be needing Irby and me for a spell, so we're fixing to leave you. But we'll be back tomorrow."

Beanie couldn't coax Tough Enough to start back to the camp with him and Irby. He petted his dog. The brothers went back along the darkening path.

Irby said, "I reckon Tough thinks there's a whole mess of Smoky Mountain bears and wildcats on this island. He figures he's got to guard the pony."

That night, as Beanie lay in a big bed with Buck and Irby, he heard stampings and snufflings outside the window. Then came a squeal.

"It's a wild pony herd!" he called out. He woke up his brothers.

From the window, in pale moonlight, he and Buck and Irby counted seven mares feeding on low-cropped grasses near the pump in the backyard. Six foals stood close to their mothers. Yearlings were frisking near the beach. A stallion was pawing a hole in the sandy soil. When water welled up, he put his thirsty mouth down and sucked.

As fast as they could, Beanie and Irby and Buck tiptoed to the back door. Buck opened it. It squeaked. The stallion snorted an alarm. Quickly the mares raised their heads. They whirled.

The stallion herded the mares and foals together. Nipping and pushing, he sent them ahead of him. All the ponies went galloping off down the beach. Their flying hoofs seemed barely to touch the sand. Manes and tails streamed out like liquid silver.

"That's the prettiest sight I ever did see," said Buck.

"Wish they'd let us get close to them," said Beanie.

Irby said, "It's only a real sick pony, that can't get away, that will let you come right close."

Back in the lumpy, creaky bed, Beanie wondered how Tough Enough and the pony were getting along.

He kept squirming restlessly. If only the night would end so he could get up and run to them…

"Quit that wiggling," said Irby. "Quit it, or we'll push you plumb out on the floor."

So Beanie kept still, and at last he went to sleep.

It was breakfast time before he knew it. "Tough Enough and Sassy!" he said to himself as he pulled on his overalls. "How are they doing now, I wonder? Reckon Tough Enough was plenty scared, waiting out the spooky dark so far from home."

After breakfast the whole family went to look at the sick pony. Tough Enough bounded to meet Beanie. He jumped on him, barking and barking away. Then he hurried back to the colt. He gave Sassy's muzzle a lick or two.

Great Grandpa put a fresh dressing in the cut he had made in the colt's hoof. He said, "Sassy's bad off, I'm telling you straight. And he won't live many days, lying down flat like that all the time. He's got to kind of sit up, or his insides won't work right."

So Pa and Buck and Irby and Beanie rolled the trunk of a fallen tree close to Sassy. They propped the pony against it and made him sit up.

Then Beanie coaxed Sassy to take food from the bottle. It held the same mixture as before, except that oats had been added.

"Go on now, Sassy," he said. "Eat it all up, you hear? Go on, now."

Pa Tatum laughed. "My soul and body! Beanie's a-nagging that pony to eat just like his ma gets after him."

"It's good to talk to a horse," said Captain Piggott, "especially to Sassy there. Sassy's mighty puny, mighty lonesome. I reckon that little bitty dog of yours knows it—knows he needs company, needs cheering up." The

Captain stopped speaking. He pulled at his pipe with sucking sounds. Then his calm voice went on again. "It stands to reason Sass knows his own herd went off and left him behind. The other horses just *had* to leave him, to look for grass and water. They had to keep on moving if they wanted to keep on living."

Beanie said, "Great Grandpa, let's make a shelter for Sass, to keep the sun and the rain off him."

Captain Piggott smiled and put his hand on Beanie's shoulder. "Sass picked himself a mighty fine shelter under this cedar tree. Don't you fret, you hear?"

After their visit to the sick pony, the young Tatums went hurrying to the beach on the ocean side of the island. Tough Enough came along, too.

"Reckon Tough needs to stretch," said Beanie, "after sticking by Sass all night."

The dog trotted to the water's edge, but he wouldn't go in. A surge of surf rushed toward him, hissing faintly as millions of tiny bubbles broke. He turned tail and ran, yip-yap-yowping.

The high waves frightened the young Tatums, too. Great Grandpa had told them to keep close to shore, out of the strong surf and the tricky undertow. So they waded in shallow water and splashed in the foamy fringes of waves. Beanie loved to feel the rush of cool strong brine round his ankles and up his legs.

He watched the black skimmers flying low over the water. The birds' beaks were open, ready to scoop up small fish. He listened to their strange, hoarse cries.

The tremendous sky of burning blue… The tremendous stretch of beach… The tremendous ocean. Beanie gazed and wondered.

There were seashells scattered all over the sand—beach pretties, the young Tatums called them. Thousands and thousands and thousands of shells: conch shells, clam shells, sand dollars, periwinkles, boat snails, whelks, scallops—shells of so many different colors, so many different shapes. Beanie and his brothers and sisters picked up as many as they could carry.

Tough Enough started to run away from the beach, toward the pony tree. He stopped and turned and barked; then he came bounding back again. He barked and barked and barked at Beanie. Off he rushed again toward the tree. He stopped again and yip-yap-yowped.

"I reckon he wants me to go back to the sick pony," said Beanie. He left his brothers and sisters and started off with the dog.

Tough Enough reached Sassy first. He touched the colt's muzzle with his nose. He looked up at Beanie and whined.

Beanie knelt down by the pony. Sassy's head was drooping low over a foreleg. Every now and then the pony gave a sort of sigh. Beanie went tight with fear. He pressed an ear against the pony's chest. He listened. At first he couldn't hear a thing. Then it came, beat-beat-beat. Sassy's heart was beating, but so faintly, it seemed to Beanie. So weakly.

"He's worse," Beanie said out loud. There was a choky lump in his throat. Salt tears stung his eyes.

Chapter Three

Beanie went running back to the camp. He asked his great grandfather to help. But Captain Piggott said, "There's nothing more I can do for the little horse. Done all I can for today. I'll change the dressing, day after tomorrow."

Great Grandma heard them talking. She came and put her arm around Beanie's shoulder. "Now don't you fret," she said. "No sick little thing, child or pony, gets well steady with nary a setback."

After supper, as usual, Beanie fed all his pets. Then he and Tough Enough went hurrying off to the pony tree. He stayed there awhile with Tough Enough and Sass. The dog lay close to the pony, pressed against him.

"You maybe got to get worse before you get better," Beanie told Sass. "When you get better, I sure wish you could live on our farm with us. Sure do."

He began to make the Tatum farm out of sand. He piled up tiny mountains and made the high valley where the Tatums lived. Then he put two little chips of driftwood close together.

"This here is our cabin," he said to Sassy, "and here's our barn."

Near the barn he placed three pebbles—the three Tatum cows. He found a big white pebble, especially nice and smooth. "Here's old Pal, our plow horse," he went on. "You'd like him, Sassy, and he'd like you. He sure would."

Beanie found some tiny snail shells to be the Tatum dogs, Sourbone and Nip and Whizz, and the Tatum cats, Cookie and Pinky Nose and Barby—the dogs and cats who had been left behind on the farm.

A tiny stick, upright in the sand near the cows, was Cousin Judd. While the Tatums were away, Cousin Judd was taking care of the animals.

"You'd get well in a hurry," Beanie said to Sass, "if you were just on our farm. Up there it's not like it is down here, all sandy and dry and hot. You'd have fresh branch water to drink, not the mean, salty stuff wild ponies get here. And sweet, thick, tender juicy grass to eat, not skimpy tough old grass. And corn—you'd get your fill of it! Pal loves it, and you would, too. You'd get fat and pert. What times we'd have together, you and Tough Enough and me! We'd chase all over the mountain meadows. You and Tough and me…"

Beanie looked at the woebegone pony. He wondered if Sassy would be better tomorrow or worse. He laid his cheek against the pony's forehead. "You got to get well. You just *got* to."

Tough Enough guarded the pony all that night. In the morning, the colt seemed better. Beanie and his brothers and sisters coaxed him to eat and drink a little. They petted him and talked to him.

The next day a small thing happened, but it was a big thing for Beanie and his brothers and sisters. When the pony heard them coming, he pricked up his ears. And his eyes looked alert as he watched them and Tough Enough.

But the day after that he slipped back. He sat still, with his eyes closed, scarcely seeming to breathe. A twitching ear, every now and then, or a slight jerk of his hide, were almost the only signs of life he gave.

Beanie felt sick at heart. He went around on the beach kicking pebbles and shells and sticks. He didn't want to join his brothers and sisters when Great Grandpa started showing them how to gig blue crabs to eat for supper. But after a while, his kicking leg got tired. He joined the others and watched and listened, and soon he speared a big crab.

Early the next morning, Captain Piggott invited the Tatums to go off on a trip in his shrimp boat, the *Lizzie Lou*. She was tied up at a pier in front of the camp. He took them out into the Sound. They fished for hogfish and croakers. Then they went over to Harkers Island, where the Piggotts had their home. While Great Grandma and Ma Tatum bought meat and groceries at a general store, the young Tatums watched fishermen mending nets. They saw men building boats.

Just as soon as they got back to Shackleford Banks, Beanie ran to see the pony. Sass nickered softly. Sudden joy made Beanie's heart almost turn over.

"Sassy likes me," Beanie told Tough Enough. "He *likes* me."

Now the pony was eating and drinking more. The swelling on his leg was down a little.

The next day Beanie took a book to the pony tree, a book that Great Grandpa had lent him. It was all about Blackbeard, a pirate whose ship had sailed nearby waters. Beanie read a chapter aloud to the dog and the pony. "I'll read some more tomorrow," he said.

After supper, Beanie combed and brushed Sassy's coat, as much of it as he could reach, with a currycomb and brush that Captain Piggott had given him.

Then he started to count the long hairs on Sassy's muzzle. When he had counted up to thirty-four, he lost his place and had to begin all over again. At last he reached a total he was sure of. Sassy had forty-seven hairs on his muzzle. Exactly forty-seven. It was important to know, Beanie felt.

Suddenly Tough Enough began to bark. He had caught sight of a sand-colored creature about as big as a saucer. It had black-button eyes, each on a sort of stalk, lifted above his head. It was a ghost crab.

Tough Enough rushed after it, barking. The crab went skittering sideways across the sand, moving with astonishing speed. When it came to a deep hole, the hole that was its home, it dived in and disappeared. Tough Enough tried to dig it out, but it was down too deep.

The next morning, when Beanie went to see Tough Enough and Sass, it was raining hard. He went splashing along the path. He liked the feel of soft mud squeezing up between his toes.

He lifted his face to the falling drops. After so many hot, dry days, he found their cool wetness good.

Rain was pelting the pony tree and dripping down on Sassy and Tough Enough. As soon as the dog saw Beanie, he started to whine.

"Quiet down," Beanie said to him. "You're not sugar. You won't melt." He began to pet him. "You never did like a bath. I reckon you need one bad, and Sass, too. Well, you're both getting one now."

He smoothed the pony's wet coat. It felt cool. "This rain will perk you up," he said.

Tough Enough was still whining when Beanie went away. The water over the path was deeper.

"Sure hope it don't rain harder," Beanie said to himself. "That hollow Sass is lying in—why, it's not much higher than this path. Only a few inches above sea level, I reckon. Water's got no place to go to, round here."

It rained steadily all that day. Every now and then Beanie would look at the water around the cottage steps. In the late afternoon, it was higher. "Maybe Tough knew a storm was coming," Beanie told himself. "Maybe that's why he was whining."

He wondered if Sassy were lying helpless in a pool that was getting deeper and deeper. He decided to go and see.

He started to run toward the pony tree, but Ma called him back. "You get in here, out of that wet," she said. "That kitty and that skunk and that coon and that crow of yours have got more sense than you've got. They're on the front porch now, out of the rain."

"Aw, Ma," Beanie begged, "I'm bad worried about Tough Enough and Sass. Let me go see how they're making out. It must be real bad, and fixing to get worse. It's the first time Fat Stuff and Sweetie Pie and Midnight was ever worrited and swiveted up enough to come up on our porch."

Ma looked at him. She said, "If it's real bad and fixing to get worse, I want you right here."

Great Grandpa and Great Grandma tried to comfort Beanie.

"It don't do no good to keep fretting yourself," said Great Grandpa. "The Coast Guard fellows are always watching for hurricanes. They'd have told us, sure, to leave the island if a real big blow was brewing."

"But what about Sass and Tough Enough?" asked Beanie. "What about *them*?"

Great Grandma said, "They'll manage. A little rain won't hurt them."

That night as Beanie lay in bed, he listened to drops drumming on the tin roof. "A little rain won't hurt them," he thought to himself, "but this here's a sure enough toad-floater."

A wind sprang up. It grew stronger. Gusts were pushing at the camp; they were striking great, soft blows. The wind churned up the waters round the island. It raised angry waves to pound the shores. Beanie had never heard them so loud. He felt strange inside.

Unhappy words went through his mind. "Tough Enough and Sass, I'm scared mighty bad for them, real bad. Those waves will get to Sass for sure, come high tide, and him lying there, too sick to move. Maybe they'll drown him."

He lay awake all night. When dawn came glimmering in, he got up. He tiptoed to a window. The rain had turned to a drizzle. Even though the tide was out, water seemed to be all around the camp. He could still hear the waves pounding the beach.

He dressed fast and tiptoed out onto the front porch. He stepped off into cold water above his ankles.

He tried to run along the trail to the pony tree, but deep pools slowed him to a walk. He was panting when he saw the tree ahead. He looked under the tree. He blinked. He looked again. A tight sound came out of his throat.

Sassy was gone. So was Tough Enough. Had waves washed them out into the Sound, carried them out at high tide?

Beanie went cold all over; he could hardly breathe. He walked toward the tree in a sort of slow daze. His dragging feet felt heavy.

All of a sudden he heard sounds. A bark. Then a soft nicker.

Happiness filled him. Warm happiness. He drew a big easy breath and then another.

On the dune, not far above, two heads were turned toward him, thrust out from behind a bush: Tough Enough's head and Sassy's head.

Beanie ran splashing through the water and up the side of the dune. Tough Enough rushed down to jump on him, to lick him, wriggling and barking.

Beanie looked at the pony once more. His eyes widened. He stared. Something had happened.

Something wonderful. Sassy was standing up! Standing on his three good legs.

Beanie gave the pony a hug. "Sass," was all he could say. The pony poked his nose against Beanie's chest.

"You're the smartest little ole pony in the world," Beanie said. "The smartest to get up here out of that deep water, and you sick and lame and all."

He noticed small tooth marks on Sassy's legs and on one of his sides. "Who's been nipping at you?" he asked.

He looked closely. The skin had not been broken. "Land's alive!" he said. "Tough Enough, I reckon it was you. When you nip me too hard, it looks just like that."

Beanie sat down on his heels and hugged the dog. "Now I know what happened," he said. "You were the one to get Sass on his feet and out of that water. You were the one who kept after him till you saved his life. I can just hear you barking and fussing at him. I can just see you nipping him. You were the one!"

Chapter Four

Sass was strong enough now to start limping along the trail toward the camp. Each day he hobbled farther, holding up his lame foot. Always Beanie led the way. He would talk and talk to the pony, "Come on, Sass, come on! You're doing just fine. Come on!"

Barking giddy-up-Sassy barks, Tough Enough would run ahead of the pony, then back and round and round him, and then ahead again.

At last, one morning, Sassy came hobbling into the camp's front yard. Both great grandparents came to see him, and all the Tatums were there. Everybody watched Sassy limp around after Tough Enough, just like another dog.

The pony seemed to know everyone was looking. He tossed his head; he arched his neck; he flirted his tail. He even kicked out weakly.

Great Grandpa chuckled. "He's trying to cut a shine."

That afternoon Captain Piggott had a talk with Pa.

The Captain didn't begin until he had sucked at his pipe. At last he said, "Your Beanie and that Tough Enough and that Sassy, seems like they rightly belong together."

"They've stuck together, and that's a true fact," said Pa.

"Well, now," said Captain Piggott, "I've had something in mind for quite a spell. I've had it in my head to give your young-uns the best pony in my herd, if you were consentable. I was thinking about a much better pony than Sassy. He's still kind of sorry looking."

The Captain lifted his pipe and pointed its stem straight at Pa. "*But*," he said, "there's good Arab blood in him. He's built right. They say a Spanish vessel with a cargo of fine horses was wrecked off this coast about three hundred years ago. The horses swam ashore, and that was the start of the wild pony herds."

"Good Arab blood or not," said Pa, "Sass just don't shape up to much."

"Exactly," said the Captain. "But that pony means a sight to Beanie and Tough Enough. So if you want to take him home with you, you're welcome to. Mighty welcome."

Pa Tatum smiled at a corner of his mouth. "Thank you kindly. Only trouble is, I can't afford to buy feed for a pet pony on our mountain farm. That Sassy, he'll always be a runt. Pal, our plow horse, will be too old to work pretty soon, and we'll put him out to pasture. But I calculate it'd take a full-size work horse to step into Pal's shoes."

Captain Piggott said nothing. Slowly, and quite carefully, he blew a big smoke ring. At last he brought out, "You'd be surprised by the job of work a Banker pony can do. A Banker pony's not really a pony, you know. He's a little horse, stunted by skimpy feed but strong as baling wire. Sassy wouldn't eat near as much as a big horse, and he'd be tougher than a big horse. A Banker pony has *got* to be tough, just to keep alive on the Banks. Sassy could pull a plow with the best of the heavy horses."

Pa Tatum scratched his head, under his thick black hair, as though trying to make himself think. He said, "Be quite a business, too, getting him home in our truck. Ma Tatum wouldn't like it at all, I reckon."

"We could fix up a box stall in your truck, easy," Captain Piggott said. "But suppose you think it over. I'd be sorry to see Beanie and Tough go home without Sass. Mighty sorry."

"I've thought it over," said Pa. His voice was kind but firm. "We just can't take the pony. I'm plumb disheartened about it."

At supper that night, Pa looked glum.

Later, when Beanie was sitting on the back steps, feeding his pets, Pa came out and stood beside him. Pa put his hand on Beanie's shoulder.

"Son," he said, "don't be getting your hopes up about taking Sassy back to our farm. The way I figure it, he just couldn't do heavy farm work."

Beanie said nothing. He looked up at Pa's face. Then he closed his eyes and lowered his head. Tough Enough seemed to know that Beanie felt sad. He put his nose on Beanie's knee and whined.

The days went by. Sassy's hollow flanks were filling with good firm flesh; his hip bones were no longer sticking out. He was limping less.

Whenever the young Tatums went swimming in the Sound, Sassy went along too. So did Tough Enough. The pony was the best swimmer of all. He would swim round and round the children and the little dog. Sometimes he went far out, and then Tough Enough would whine and bark and bark after him in a come-back-Sassy way.

Once, when Sass was headed away from shore, the dog got hold of his tail and tried to pull him back. But the pony kept going. Tough Enough had to let go and swim for the beach.

Beanie taught Sassy to wear a halter. At the start of the first lesson, Buck and Irby held the pony while Beanie put on an old halter Great Grandpa had given him. Sass didn't seem to mind. He just shook his head a few times.

Beanie slipped a long rope into his halter ring. Gently, slowly, he began to guide him. Pretty soon he was leading him around. He loved to lead him.

He gave him things to eat that were new to him. But, little by little, bite by bite, he grew to like them. It wasn't long before he was eating them eagerly.

Sometimes, though, he nibbled at things he wasn't supposed to nibble at. One day, Beanie went to his mother and asked her to sew on a button.

"Give me the button," she said, and held out her hand.

"I don't know where it got to," said Beanie. "Sassy pulled it plumb off my overalls. He kind of chewed it. Then he spit it out, I reckon, or maybe he swallowed it. Anyhow, it's gone."

So Ma had to use a safety pin. And it wasn't long before Irby had lost two buttons. Sassy pulled a button off Serena, too, but she got it back from him and sewed it on herself. Then Buck lost a button, and so did Annie Mae.

"I declare!" said Ma. "That's the button-pullingest pony!"

Great Grandpa had to take her over to Harkens Island in his shrimp boat to buy buttons and buttons and buttons.

One morning Beanie saw a red place on the skin of the colt's left hind foot, just at the upper edge of the hoof. It was almost hidden by long coarse hair. He told Captain Piggott.

With his pocket knife, the Captain cut into the hoof, this time from above. He pulled out a sliver of shell. "Just what I suspicioned," he said.

"There it is, Sassy Boy!" Beanie cried. "The thing that's been hurting and hurting you so long. You're going to be fine, just fine."

Beanie was so happy that, after dinner, he gave Tough Enough and Sass part of his dessert, each a little helping of vanilla ice cream that Great Grandma had made. Both ate it up in a quick, smacking way.

Next time the Piggotts and Tatums had ice cream for dinner, Sassy smelled it. He came to the back door. He snorted and he pawed the ground. But nobody brought him ice cream.

Two steps led up into the cottage. Sassy tried them out, tap-tapping with a hoof—the first step, then the second. His teeth pulled at the button-shaped door knob till the screen door opened slightly. Then he opened the door wider by sticking a front foot in.

Next his head poked in, and then all the rest of him. His feet made dry little knocking noises as he walked into the kitchen and to the table where all the Tatums were sitting with Great Grandpa and Great Grandma.

Pa Tatum's biggest laugh came bursting. "Gol*eee*!" he said. "That little fellow's real sociable-like, dogged if he ain't."

Ma Tatum's lips went thin. "It's his stomach that's sociable-like," she said. "It wants to be where the ice cream is. Beanie Tatum, you quit feeding that critter our vittles. Next time we have fried chicken, I don't want him sitting up alongside me, a-gnawing on a drumstick."

Everybody began to laugh—everybody but Ma. She said, "Beanie Tatum, you get that horse right out of this house."

Beanie led the pony out and tethered him to a tree with his halter rope. As soon as he had gone, the pony's teeth went to work on the rope. Sassy gnawed it and bit it and jerked at it until, at last, it broke. Once more he went stepping into the cottage.

Everybody laughed and laughed, even Ma Tatum, this time.

Beanie hadn't finished his second big helping of vanilla ice cream. He took his dish outside the cottage and set it down. The pony followed him in a hurry. Tough Enough came running to help Sass eat the ice cream.

So, whenever the Piggotts and the Tatums were going to have ice cream, Great Grandma made a generous extra helping. Beanie would set a big dish of it near the back steps, for Sassy. Tough Enough always helped him to eat it up.

By this time, Sass was running around as if he had never come close to death. He still limped, but the limp was so slight that it was hardly a limp at all.

Beanie had an idea. He thought it would be fun if he could teach Sass to come to him. But, he wondered, how could he do it? At last he hit on a plan.

Every time he fed the pony, he whistled three short whistles. Sassy learned that those whistles meant a meal. He would come trotting fast.

But trouble began when Midnight, the crow, started to imitate Beanie. One morning he flew up and down the beach, whistling Beanie's whistles. And up and down, up and down, Sassy went trotting after him.

"You pesky old crow, you!" Beanie shouted, but he couldn't help laughing.

Tough Enough started off along the beach so fast that his legs were a blur. He was chasing Sass. He seemed to know there was something wrong when a horse kept obeying a bird's whistles.

Beanie yelled, "Hey, Tough! Get Sass! Go get him, go get him!"

The dog caught up with Sassy. He nudged the pony's forelegs with his nose and nipped them a little. He headed the pony off and made him turn and run back toward Beanie. He barked a lot of giddy-up-Sassy barks.

Pretty soon Sass was nuzzling Beanie's neck. Beanie patted and petted him and the dog. He led them back to the camp and got an apple for Sassy and a scrap of meat for Tough Enough.

So, after that, the dog brought the pony to Beanie whenever Beanie told him to.

The first time Pa Tatum saw Tough Enough's new trick he threw back his head and laughed. "It plumb tickles me," he said. "Just listen to him go after Sassy like a sheep dog fetching a sheep. He sure is a managing hound."

One day Irby said to Beanie, "Let's make a sled for Sass to pull, the kind of sled we haul logs out of the woods with, back home. I know how to do it, sort of, and Pa said he'd help us."

They began to make the sled. They built it out of driftwood and out of planks from a wrecked ship stranded on the beach. They sawed and whittled and hammered away. When the sled was finished, both brothers looked at it proudly.

Captain Piggott gave them an old harness, with a singletree, for the pony. He said, "Better make Sass acquainted with the harness and the sled kind of gradual-like. Mind you, let him look at them and sniff them right at the start. Do that, and they won't mommuck him any."

So that was what Beanie and Irby did. Sassy didn't like the bit at first. He chewed at it and pawed at it. But Beanie talked to him and stroked him.

As time went on, the pony got used to both harness and sled. Beanie and Irby taught him to pull the sled across firm damp sand near the water's edge. Tough Enough helped him learn. The dog would run close to the pony, barking his giddy-up-Sassy barks and nipping at Sassy's heels. The brothers would take turns riding behind the pony. If too many got on the sled,

Sass would make a jerky turn. The sled would go up on its side and dump them into the water.

Sometimes Sass would join a herd of wild ponies—Captain Piggott's herd. Kicking and squealing, he would frisk around with other yearlings. It seemed to be a sort of game. "Playing horse tag." That was what the Captain called it.

Always, when that game was going on, Beanie had to hold his dog by the collar. Tough Enough would have chased the herd away. He would whine and whimper till Sassy came loping back.

Chapter Five

The hot late-July days drowsed along. Yucca plants on the Sound side of the island were lifting their green swords and holding their snowy, bell-shaped blossoms high. Close to the ground, wild Cherokee roses spread their simple petals to the sun.

Half of the summer was gone. It was almost time for the Tatums to go back to their farm so they could start all the canning they had to do.

All the young Tatums helped stow bundles and boxes on board the Captain's shrimp boat floating alongside the pier.

The beach pretties were part of the baggage. The children put them in sacks and paper bags they called pokes. There were pokes of pebbles, of coral, of starfish—pokes full of shells and pokes tight with seaweed. There were even pokes heavy with clean, white, treasured sand.

At feeding time, the evening before the Tatums' going-away day, Beanie put Midnight in his cage. He put on Fat Stuff's collar, and Sweetie Pie's. With the raccoon's chain and the skunk's leash, he tied up the animals indoors. He didn't want to leave them, or the crow, on this island where great hurricanes might strike.

Beanie and His Pony

Next morning, everybody was up long before dawn. Work began by the yellow light of lanterns.

As the Tatums worked, Sassy kept trotting about, with Tough Enough following close. He seemed restless and uneasy. He was all over the place, sniffing at bundles, walking from one person to another, pulling at buttons.

Beanie and Irby and Annie Mae and Serena put Beanie's pets on the shrimp boat: Sweetie Pie, Midnight, Bobcat Bob, and Fat Stuff—all but Tough Enough.

Now Beanie knew it was time. Time to say goodbye to Sassy Boy. He put his hand on the pony's neck. He stroked it. But he couldn't say a word.

He stooped and picked up Tough Enough. He carried the dog into the boat, to the stern. In his arms, Tough Enough whined and wriggled, twisting himself around, trying to see Sassy. The pony stood at the edge of the shore, looking at the boat. He nickered.

Beanie's mouth twisted. Tears filled his eyes. He winked and winked them away.

Great Grandpa started the engine. Pa and Buck cast off the ropes that tied the boat to the pier. Slowly the boat began to move away from the shore.

Beanie was still holding on to Tough Enough. He was afraid the dog would jump right out of the boat. Tough Enough started to howl. There was another whinny from Sass, and another. Then the whinnying stopped.

Beanie heard Captain Piggott say, "I got her at half speed. The channel's tricky, changing all the time, mess of shoals hereabouts."

The shrimp boat kept parting the Sound's calm waters. Lights on far shores gleamed brightly; their reflections floated long and shimmering. Buoys made lonesome noises. A beam from a lighthouse kept slashing the sky. In the east, a faint gray light was slowly spreading. Early dawn had come.

All of a sudden, Tough Enough began to bark. He strained against Beanie's arms and chest. He pointed his nose toward the dark waters behind the boat.

"Something's happened," Beanie cried out. "Tough's barking his *something's-happened* barks."

Captain Piggott peered into the dimness. He slowed the shrimp boat. "Hush that dog up!" he said to Beanie. "I can't hear a thing with him making such a ruckus. If anybody's in trouble, I want to hear him holler."

Beanie put his hand over Tough Enough's muzzle and held the dog's mouth shut. Tough Enough wriggled violently. He made glugging, choking noises in his throat. He pawed and pawed at Beanie's hand.

The Captain lifted his voice in a hail: "Ahoy there!" Nobody answered. "Ahoy, ahoy, ahoy!" the Captain shouted again and again.

"There he is!" yelled Beanie. He pointed to a dark spot. It was moving slowly toward the stern of the shrimp boat. Captain Piggott stopped the boat. Beanie saw a long, dark-brown head.

"It's Sassy!" he cried out. He forgot to keep holding on to Tough Enough's muzzle. The dog began a shrill barking. He was barking his giddy-up-Sassy barks.

"It's Sass!" shrieked Annie Mae.

"Sass!" yelled Irby.

"Little Sass," said Buck.

"Sassy Boy!" said Serena.

Ma and Pa didn't say a thing. Neither did Great Grandpa or Great Grandma.

The Captain started the boat. She was moving again toward Harkers Island, but more slowly this time.

Beanie ran to Captain Piggott. He still had Tough Enough in his arms. He made the dog stop barking.

"Sassy'll drown for sure, Great Grandpa!" he cried. "Can't we get him aboard? Can't we?"

"Now don't you mommuck yourself," said the Captain. "We got no way of getting a horse aboard. But we're more than halfway to Harkers Island. No use heading back toward the camp. That pony's a strong swimmer, mighty strong, and he's got all kinds of sense. I reckon he'll make out all right. Why, I've heard of Banker ponies swimming five miles or more, and it can't be more than two and a half miles from Shackleford Banks across to Harkers Island. We'll kind of ease along at the pony's swimming speed—and just wait and see."

The Captain pointed at Tough Enough. "You've got that dog to put spirit into the pony and make Sassy do his best. Remember that."

Now all the Tatums and Great Grandma were close to the stern of the boat. They were watching Sassy and calling out to him. They could see him clearly, now, in the strengthening light.

Pa put his hand on Beanie's shoulder. His voice came gruff and strange. "Son, I reckon I was wrong. If Sassy can make it to shore, we'll—we'll take him back to the farm."

"Oh, *Pa!*" said Beanie. He wanted to jump and shout. He squeezed Tough Enough so hard that the dog gave a yelp.

Pa said, "If Sassy's stout enough to swim the Sound, he'll be stout enough to pull a plow, most likely. But, puller or not, we'll take him along. The little fellow's got gumption."

Ma nodded. "Reckon it ain't no use a-going against nature. It's natural for that boy and that dog to keep a-getting hold of critters, one way or the other."

"Come on, Sassy Boy!" Beanie shouted.

Slowly, steadily, the little horse was pushing through the water. His eyes had a strained look in them. They were staring at the shrimp boat.

To Beanie the Sound seemed as wide as the ocean itself. Could Sassy ever reach the shore? The pony had dropped farther behind. He was getting tired. Captain Piggott slowed the boat.

Beanie turned quickly. He gazed toward Harkers Island. Not far ahead was the end of a narrow pier, the pier in front of the Piggotts' home.

Then Beanie looked back toward the pony. He yelled, "You've made it, Sassy Boy—almost." But suddenly he could no longer see Sassy. Where the pony had been, there were only ripples and bubbles.

Then a head, long and dripping, pushed up above the surface. Sassy gave a loud snort as he blew water out of his nose. Once more he began to swim, but slowly and quite feebly.

He stopped. At last his feet had touched bottom. He staggered toward the beach. Pretty soon he sank down in water a few inches deep, his head up, his nostrils wide, his sides heaving with quick, short breaths.

Tough Enough and Beanie jumped out of the boat as soon as it nudged the pier, even before Pa and Buck had made it fast. Close behind them, in a scramble, came Irby and Serena and Annie Mae.

Tough Enough rushed toward Sass, and all the others followed. In a moment the dog was splashing round and round Sassy, barking and barking away. Then he jumped up again and again to lick the colt's nose. Beanie threw his arms round Sassy's neck. The other young Tatums were petting and patting the pony.

"Sass," Beanie choked out the word, "you're our pony now, Tough Enough's and mine."

Sassy gave a nicker. He lurched to his feet. He followed Tough Enough and the children up the beach to the Piggotts' front yard. There he began to nibble at the grass and clover in the greenest part of the lawn.

Great Grandma brought Beanie some old towels, and he wiped the pony dry.

The other young Tatums began to unload the shrimp boat and carry ashore the pets and pokes and bundles and boxes.

In the backyard, the Tatums' old truck was waiting patiently. Pa Tatum and Great Grandpa drove to a boat yard nearby and bought some old planks for a ramp so Sassy could walk up it into the truck.

After they came back, they measured and sawed and hammered, with Buck and Irby and Beanie helping. At last the ramp was ready.

All this time the other Tatums had been loading their truck. To make room for Sass, they had tied some of the bundles outside and overhead.

Inside the truck, Pa and Great Grandpa made wooden slots to hold the ramp upright so it could be a partition, one side of Sassy's box stall, once the pony was in.

Then they put the ramp in place behind the truck.

Slowly, very slowly, Sassy went up, snorting and tapping his way along. Beanie was leading him and talking to him. Tough Enough was urging him on with yips and yowps and little nips. At last the pony was safely in.

Pa and Buck pulled the ramp inside the truck. They fitted it into its wooden slots.

The pony was standing in his stall. Little shivers shook him. His coat was moist with sweat. He gave a squealing whinny.

Beanie patted his damp back. "Reckon you think you're cooped up in a crate," he said gently. "But don't you be afraid."

Tough Enough was standing right under Sassy's head. His tail was wagging, his tongue was out, and his mouth was open almost in a smiling way. He kept looking up at Sassy.

The pony lowered his muzzle. He and the dog touched noses. Sassy began to calm down.

Pa Tatum eyed him. He grinned. "Little fellow, we'll pick up hay and oats for you on the way."

Great Grandma and Great Grandpa were standing close to the truck. Beanie had never seen them look so sad. All the Tatums gathered round them.

Now there was a feeling. It showed in everybody's faces. It seemed to be in the air. It was a feeling of farewell.

After a lot of goodbye kissing, Great Grandma wiped her eyes. "It does beat all," she said, "how the time has flown. Why, it seems like you all just got here."

"We're going to miss you all, bad," Great Grandpa said.

There was a heavy silence. Sudden noises broke it—three throaty calls from Midnight, the crow. "Hey, hey, hey!" the bird squawked.

Everybody laughed.

The Tatums climbed into the truck. Pa smiled at one side of his mouth. He looked half pleased, half worried. "Every*body* that's going is in," he said, "and every*thing* and every *critter*. So now we'd best put out to go, before we take on anything else and split plumb open."

Crr-r-r, crr-r-r. That was the starter grinding away. *Cough-cough-cough.* That was the truck's motor starting.

"Goodbye!" shouted Great Grandpa and Great Grandma, again and again.

"Goodbye!" shouted all the Tatums, over and over and over. The truck was jouncing along the bumpy lane that led to the smooth westward road.

The Tatums were on their way.

More Books from The Good and the Beautiful Library!

Lions in the Barn
by Virginia Voight

Juddie
by Florence Wightman Rowland

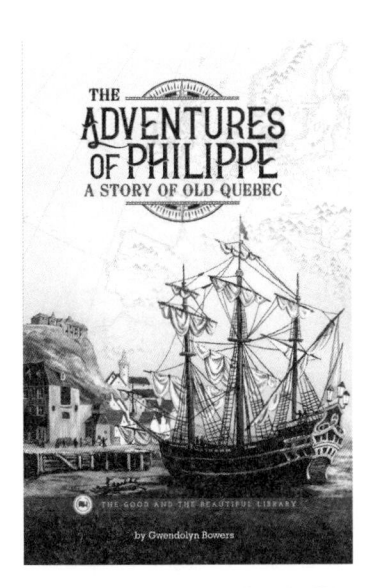

The Adventures of Phillipe
by Gwendolyn Bowers

*Toby Has a Dog
and Other Books by May Justus*
by May Justus

www.thegoodandthebeautiful.com